COMING TWO MY EYES

Arief Abdullah Tan

Contents

lovingly dedicated to…

Azura: Just like with my first book, you can point the finger at my wife if this one offends your intelligence. After more than 23 years together, I guess this is her subtle revenge plot. Her patience and tolerance with my endless writing escapades are truly commendable. Or perhaps she's just plotting for a bestseller to buy herself a getaway from my quirks!

Adam: My son's antics have delayed the completion of this book more times than I can count, but he has been a delightful addition to our family. His quirky sense of humor, cunning mischief, and wisdom far beyond his years are qualities I wouldn't trade for all the peace in the world. Who needs tranquility when you can have a daily dose of laughter and a masterclass in creative chaos?

Mom and Mom-in-law: Though they carried their regrets in this world, they left us with hearts full of gratitude. Their legacy of love and knowledge will forever guide us and inspire Adam and beyond.

Above all, to our Creator: For granting me the opportunity to live, love, and learn more of His wonderful blessings each day. Here's to the divine scriptwriter of our lives, who always keeps the plot twists coming!

author's thoughts

THIS masterpiece (or pieces once you decide to tear it up) is only 14 years overdue. Like my first book, the hardest part of writing this wasn't the lack of inspiration.

No, the hardest part was explaining to everyone why there wasn't a second book after the "success" of my first one. I guess selling three copies is a bit too far-fetched to call a success.

"Dad, why haven't you written another book?" my son asked.

I could say I lacked ideas, was perpetually lazy, and was always busy. Or that I spent so much time waiting for his school bell to ring, finishing his tuition classes, and attending his football games, badminton matches, and taekwondo sessions that I just couldn't find the time.

The truth was that I finally realized the hot soccer moms and badminton Makciks were not interested in my attempts to socialize. I blamed it on my unrecognizable literary credentials.

But isn't it funny how life's journey can be so consuming that we forget about what really matters?

We get caught up in the daily grind, the routines, the endless tasks that fill our calendars, and we lose sight of the passions and dreams we once held dear.

It's like we're on this endless treadmill, going nowhere fast, while the things that truly make life meaningful slip further and further out of reach.

So, without hesitation, I approached the sanitized keyboard and started typing with purpose. Also, I still had about seven hours to go before I could log off from work.

rain man (and woman)

THE thunderstorm was on something fierce and throwing a wild party. It wasn't just pouring cats and dogs; it was more like a full-blown animal kingdom descending from the sky.

Struggling to see past the four-wheel drive's windscreen, Zarinah decided it was time to pull over before she became part of the zoo parade outside.

"Let's see what the next stop is. Probably just a quaint, rotting little food stall," the 45-year-old divorcee muttered to herself.

Zarinah Rashid was once a superstar in the world of journalism, known for her fearless reporting and relentless pursuit of the truth. But after a messy divorce and a string of personal and professional disasters, she was now jobless, cynical, and thoroughly disillusioned.

Much like the storm she and her car were battling, she felt lost and adrift, unsure where to go next and struggling to come to terms with the way her life had spun off course.

Five kilometers behind, spinning was exactly what football coach Reevan James was desperately trying to avoid. His 20-year-old but trusty red Harley motorcycle was losing the battle to stay upright in the downpour.

Drenched and squinting through the unforgiving wind pelting his chiseled face, he hunted for a place to stop. If he had bothered to check Waze or the meteorological department's app, he could have planned his stops earlier.

But the 52-year-old had an aversion to technology, gadgets, and phones. He longed for the simplicity of the past when the only connections were face-to-face, heart-to-heart, and dial-up internet at best.

Aiden Koh was the complete opposite. Gadgets, mobile phones, and round-the-clock internet access were the story of his life. Not like any of these things can help him get out of this storm either.

Struggling to floor the pedal down on his freshly minted Tesla, Waze was showing the

25-year-old rich brat the next available place to stop ahead.

"Kampung Ketiak?" Why would anyone name a village after armpits?"

It had been over three hours since their paths collided at the village's only convenience store, a small, dusty shop crammed with forgotten trinkets and memories no one remembered.

The storm had dwindled to a steady rain. While it had been a full-on zoo earlier, it now felt more like a mini petting farm. The air was thick with the scent of incense and old paper from within the shop.

The owner, Kak Wan a wizened old woman with eyes that held the secrets of the universe, spoke little but smiled knowingly at the three strangers.

She saw something within them that they couldn't, or maybe she had just binged Korean horror flicks on Netflix all week and was now seeing ghosts everywhere.

"Where are you headed after this, Coach?" Zarinah asked.

Reevan found her an enigma. A city girl dressed in clothes that seemed too tight and too revealing for the village, with a frown that could curdle milk.

"Headed back to KL," he replied.

"Looking forward to a hot shower and some fresh clothes. Right now, I smell like a biology experiment," he chuckled.

Zarinah raised an eyebrow. "Nice to know you're still functional. I thought your brain might have fried along with your phone."

Reevan laughed. "Touché. And you? Heading back to the city to find out why your plants keep dying?"

She smirked. "Something like that. Or maybe just to remember why city life stresses me out."

The store owner nodded as if she understood, or she was just agreeing with the dramatic plot twist in her head.

"You both need more tea," she said, handing them each a cup. "Or maybe a good raincoat."

Aiden let out a tiny but audible laugh, his first reaction since their odd trio had formed in the shop.

Kak Wan looked at him and exclaimed, "Alamak, he is alive!"

Reevan and Zarinah exchanged glances, both thinking the same thing: This village wasn't so bad after all.

Just then, the clouds darkened, and the skies turned gloomy again. They weren't going anywhere anytime soon.

chicken little (or none)

AS they weaved their way earlier through the winding roads leading to Kampung Ketiak, Zarinah couldn't help but raise an eyebrow at the village's peculiar name.

"Kampung Ketiak? Sounds like we're nestled snugly under someone's underarms," she remarked dryly, earning a chuckle from Reevan.

With a heavy sigh, Zarinah recounted her latest misadventure in Singapore, her dreams of corporate success crumbling like a poorly constructed Jenga tower.

"Well, that job interview was a royal disaster. I think I set a record for awkward silence," she grumbled, kicking a pebble along the dusty floor.

Aiden, oblivious to the palpable tension, was engrossed in his phone, his thumbs dancing across the screen with practiced precision.

"You're quite the celebrity, Zarinah. Google practically rolls out the red carpet for your search results," he quipped, barely lifting his gaze.

"Super glue manufacturers would kill for that level of adhesion."

Rolling her eyes, Zarinah shot back, "Yeah, well, fame and a couple of bucks will get me a cup of coffee. Not exactly the success story I was aiming for."

Over the next half hour, Aiden launched into an impromptu crash course on LinkedIn and job apps on the phone, his fingers flying across the keyboard like a virtuoso pianist.

Despite his digital prowess, Reevan saw that there was a flicker of longing in his eyes, as if the young lad too yearned for a connection beyond the glowing screen of his smartphone.

As the vintage clock in the village square chimed eight times, its rhythmic pendulum swaying in hypnotic motion, the trio found themselves swept up in the tranquil ambiance of the village.

"Feels like time slows down in this place," Reevan mused, taking in the serene surroundings.

"Or maybe it's just the clock struggling to keep up with its pendulum."

With a gentle nudge from the shop owner, the trio ventured deeper into the heart of Kampung Ketiak, greeted by the warm smiles of its residents.

"It's like stepping into a scene from The Waltons," Zarinah remarked, a wry smile tugging at her lips. "Minus the overalls and folksy wisdom, of course."

Pak Wahab was the operator of the village's sole diner. Dinner time was the highlight of his day. His rickety shop somehow managed to surprisingly fit in the whole village's population.

There was no menu, and Pak Wahab and his frail-looking assistant did not ask us what we wanted. We were served a plate of mixed rice with white rice, fried chicken, fried egg, and sambal belacan. The default drink was an overly sweet sirap bandung.

As we settled down, Zarinah, ever the demanding one, nudged Reevan. "Can you ask them if they have any vegetarian options?" she said, looking down at her plate with mild disdain.

Reevan sighed. "As you can tell, no menu means we eat what we're given."

"But I don't eat chicken," Zarinah insisted.

The coach muttered under his breath, before turning to Pak Wahab's assistant, who was bustling around the tiny space. He whispered as quietly as possible.

The assistant, who looked like a gust of wind could knock him over, blinked at Reevan. "Vegetarian? You mean, no chicken?" he asked loudly.

"Yes, no chicken," Reevan confirmed, nodding.

The assistant scratched his head and yelled out to Pak Wahab. "Pak Wahab, tak nak ayam!"

The chef, a sturdy man with a perpetual smile, glanced over and laughed heartily. "No chicken? In my shop? That's like asking for rain in the desert!"

The whole diner erupted in laughter, and even Aiden couldn't help but laugh.

Zarinah, however, was undeterred. "What about just rice and vegetables? Surely that's possible?"

Pak Wahab sauntered over, still chuckling. "Ah, you city folks and your strange ways. We have what we have. Maybe tomorrow, bring your own veggies, and I'll cook them for you."

As the evening wore on, the villagers chatted and laughed, sharing stories, and enjoying their meals. Even Zarinah seemed to relax, joining in the laughter.

For the first time in what felt like ages, Zarinah allowed herself to be present in the moment. She couldn't remember the last time she had felt so at ease and genuinely laughed. Back home, she was always flustered, perpetually caught up in the chaos of her thoughts.

Lately, the sting of failure had only added to her stress. After being retrenched from her last job, she had been unable to land a new position. The rejections felt like personal affronts, and she couldn't shake the suspicion that her age played a significant role.

This constant struggle had left her angry all the time. Her frustration spilled over into every aspect of her life, making it hard to find joy in anything.

Yet here, amidst the warmth and camaraderie of the village, something shifted. The simplicity and sincerity of the villagers' interactions began to soothe her troubled mind.

Pak Wahab's diner might not have had a menu, but it had something much more valuable: a sense of community and a lot of heart.

bend it like aiden

AIDEN slumped into the chair of his tiny office; a small cubicle tucked away in the back corner of his dad's property development company. His fingers hovered over the keyboard, hesitating to type yet another mundane tweet about a new condominium project.

The walls felt like they were closing in, adorned with dull blueprints and brochures, all serving as a reminder of the path he was too afraid to stray from.

The door burst open, and in walked Jack, carrying a football under his arm.

"Mate, you look like you've been tackled by a truck. What's up?"

Aiden sighed. "Just the usual. Another day, another hashtag. I feel like I'm playing in a game with no goalposts."

His voice carried a note of resignation, mirroring the monotony that had settled into his daily routine. As the company's social media manager, Aiden was responsible for creating digital campaigns and social media activities to drive sales for the company's development projects.

On paper, it sounded dynamic and exciting, but the reality felt far removed from that promise.

Aiden had been thrust into this position by his dad immediately after completing university. There had been no discussion, no exploration of his interests or passions, just an unspoken expectation that he would slot into the family business.

He recalled the conversation with his father after graduation.

"Dad, I've been thinking a lot about my future, and I don't want to work at the company. I appreciate the opportunity, but my passion lies in creative photography.

His father frowned, the lines on his forehead deepening. "Aiden, you need to be practical. Photography is a hobby, not a career. The company needs you, and it's a stable, respectable job."

Aiden's heart pounded in his chest, but he pressed on. "I understand that, but photography isn't just a hobby for me. It's what I love. I want to build a career out of it, even if it means starting from scratch and facing challenges."

His father sighed heavily, the sound filled with a mixture of frustration and even a tinge of disappointment.

"You're young and idealistic. The real world doesn't work like that. You have responsibilities, and you need to think about your future security. Working for the company ensures that."

"Stop dreaming!" his father snapped, his voice growing sharper.

"As the eldest, it is your duty to take over the business one day. You will take care of your younger sisters and secure their future as well. This isn't a choice, Aiden, it's your responsibility."

That was the end of the conversation.

The pressure to meet these expectations weighed heavily on Aiden, squeezing out any enthusiasm he might have once had for the role. Every morning, he sat at his desk, scrolling through trending topics, brainstorming catchy slogans, and curating images that he hoped would capture the fleeting attention of potential customers.

Yet, despite his efforts, it all felt hollow. He couldn't shake the feeling that he was merely going through the motions, a cog in a machine that cared little for his aspirations.

Aiden's mind often drifted to what could have been. He had dreams of traveling, exploring different cultures, and perhaps even pursuing a career that ignited his passion.

He longed for something more, something that made him feel alive and purposeful. But for now, he was stuck in this cycle, unsure of how to break free and find a path that truly resonated with who he was and who he wanted to be.

His acne-filled colleague chuckled, plopping down in the chair across from Aiden. "Well, I've got news for you. Every game has goalposts. Sometimes you just can't see them because you're stuck defending."

The young heir to Mr. Koh's business empire raised an eyebrow. "Defending? I'm not even in the game. I'm just sitting on the sidelines."

"Exactly!" Jack leaned forward, eyes twinkling with enthusiasm. "You're on the sidelines of your own life. It's time to get on the pitch and start playing forward."

Jack, a fervent Liverpool fan, tossed the ball to Aiden, who caught it instinctively. "Listen, your dad's not the referee of your dreams. You are. He might own the team, but you control how you play. Think of it like football. Every player starts in the youth academy, right?"

"Yeah, but they usually want to be there," Aiden replied, rolling the ball between his hands.

"You always make it sound so simple. And you sound exactly like Coach Reevan."

It has been over three months since their drenching encounter at Kampung Ketiak. The football coach then said something similar back at Pak Wahab's shop.

"Look, when I coach the kids, I tell them they need to find their position. Some are strikers, some are defenders. You're a striker, Aiden."

Reevan's words gave Aiden a flicker of hope. "You've got a passion for wildlife photography that could score goals, but you're stuck playing defense in your office."

At that time, the tranquility of the jungle and the simplicity of the village amplified Reevan's message. His words seemed so enlightened.

Turning back to his pal, Aiden asked, "But how do I switch positions without getting benched?"

Jack grinned. "You need a game plan. Start training on the side. Build your portfolio like a player builds their skills."

"Show your dad that you're serious about nature photography. He might be traditional, but even he can appreciate a well-executed play."

"And what if he doesn't?" Aiden asked, anxiety creeping back into his voice. He has been grudgingly doing his job for the last three years.

"Then you keep playing your game," Jack said firmly. "In football, sometimes you must take a shot even if you're not sure it'll go in. You miss 100% of the shots you don't take."

"What's the worst that can happen? He yells at you. You're already afraid of that. Might as well give him a real reason."

Aiden laughed, feeling lighter than he had in years. "You make it sound like facing a defender isn't so bad."

Jack winked. "It's all about perspective. A defender's just another obstacle. You learn to maneuver around them. Every great player faces tough opponents. It's how you grow."

Determination replaced his earlier gloom. "Alright. Let's do it! Maybe I'll sneak in some nature photos on the company's social media. But where can I go to take nature shots?"

the jungle book

ZARINAH sat at the kitchen table, sipping her lukewarm coffee as she scrolled through yet another rejection email from a news outlet. The bitterness of the coffee mirrored her feelings toward the industry that had once embraced her but now deemed her 'too old' and 'outdated'.

She clenched her fists, frustration bubbling inside her like a volcano ready to erupt. Her children, Ziana and Zakaria, walked into the kitchen, immediately sensing their mother's mood.

Ziana, the older of the two at 15, placed a gentle hand on her mom's shoulder. "Don't be upset. You'll find something soon."

Zakaria, 12 years old and wise beyond his years, chimed in, "Yeah, Mom. You're the best writer ever. They're just blind if they can't see that."

Zarinah managed a weak smile, grateful for their unwavering support.

"Thanks, darlings. It's just... frustrating. I used to be on top of the world in journalism, and now it feels like I'm chasing shadows."

Ziana sat down beside her mother, concern etching her features. "Have you thought about freelancing? Or maybe starting a blog?"

Zarinah sighed, shaking her head. "I have. But it's not the same. I want to make an impact again, like I did with that series on urban legends. Remember?"

Zakaria's eyes lit up. "Yeah! That was epic! Everyone at school was talking about it."

Zarinah's feature on urban legends had been a high point in her journalism career. It wasn't just another article; it was a deep dive into the mysteries and folklore that had fascinated people for generations.

She meticulously researched and uncovered tales that were both chilling and captivating, drawing readers into a world where the line between reality and myth blurred. Each story was carefully crafted, blending historical facts with the eerie elements of the legends, making readers question what they thought they knew about their cities.

The series included detailed accounts of ghostly apparitions in abandoned buildings, eerie occurrences in historic sites, and whispered tales of supernatural encounters that had been passed down through generations.

Zarinah didn't just recount these stories; she visited the locations, interviewed witnesses, and even consulted experts in folklore and paranormal activities.

Her narrative style was gripping, combining the thrill of a horror story with the investigative rigor of a journalist. The feature series garnered widespread acclaim, not just for its content, but for Zarinah's ability to breathe life into old tales and present them in a way that felt both fresh and authentic.

The urban legend series sparked conversations and debates, and even inspired a local television show. It had cemented Zarinah's reputation as a storyteller who could captivate an audience and bring forgotten stories to light.

Zarinah's heart warmed at the memory. "Exactly. I want to do something like that again. Something big. Something that shakes people out of their complacency."

Ziana pondered for a moment. "What about Kampung Ketiak? You've been talking about it for months."

Zarinah froze, the mention of the small village bringing a flood of memories rushing back.

The boy leaned forward eagerly. "So, go back! Find out more. Maybe that's your big story!"

Zarinah looked at her children, their faces glowing with hope. She felt a surge of determination she hadn't felt in a long time.

"You know what? You're right. The village might just hold the key to my comeback."

A week later, armed with her well-traveled compact camera and a notebook; she might be the only person on earth still using these, Zarinah set off for the village she had accidentally driven into. The drive was long, far from the bustling city where she once thrived.

As she approached, memories of her previous visit flooded back: the hushed yet friendly villagers, the quaint wooden houses, and the air thick with unspoken stories.

She parked near the convenience store, where Kak Wan the shop owner was on her customary bench taking a nap under the shade of an ancient tree.

Zarinah took a deep breath, feeling a renewed sense of purpose. For her, this wasn't just about relaunching her career. It was about reclaiming her voice, about showing her children that resilience and passion can conquer any obstacle.

With a smile on her face and a notebook full of untold stories, Zarinah started walking toward Kan Wan.

school of rocks

KAK Wan was not too forthcoming with stories about the village. For most of Zarinah's questions, she simply nodded and said, "Nothing much to write about."

After two hours of digging, the award-winning journalist had hit a roadblock on what more to ask. The village seemed like a place where time had stood still, yet somehow also faded away.

Boring village. About 50 people left staying there. Mostly fruit farmers and others worked in the nearby bigger townships as lorry drivers and farm hands. In the 1980s, there had been increased attention for its dense jungles. Outsiders used to come into the jungles to search for elephants and wild boars.

Today, it was only the residents and, on exceedingly rare occasions, people who stopped by to use the washroom or to shelter from the rain.

Zarinah felt a pang of frustration as she clicked her pen and snapped her notebook shut. Her mind was buzzing with the incomplete narrative of this uneventful village. She had a reputation for uncovering hidden gems in the most unassuming places, but here, she felt like she was trying to draw blood from a stone.

Kak Wan noticed the change in Zarinah's demeanor. "You look tired," she said, her voice gentle and grandmotherly.

"I guess I am," Zarinah replied, offering a tired smile.

"I thought there would be more to write about. Every place has its story, right?"

Kak Wan nodded slowly, her eyes distant. "Maybe you're looking in the wrong places."

Zarinah raised an eyebrow, but before she could probe further, Kak Wan excused herself to tend to her chores. Zarinah sighed, watching the elderly woman shuffle away. The village was quaint, with its wooden houses on stilts and lush greenery, but it lacked the vibrancy she sought.

As she packed her things and prepared to leave, something curious hit her. In those two hours, she had not seen or heard any children around the village. No crying toddlers, no kids running around, no school kids kicking anything.

The realization made her pause. How could she have missed something so glaringly obvious?

Zarinah decided to take a walk around the village once more. She strolled past the rows of wooden houses, peering into open doorways and yards. She saw adults engaged in their daily routines, tending to gardens, repairing fishing nets, or simply sitting on their porches, but there was no sign of any children.

She approached a group of women who were sitting under a large mango tree, chatting, and peeling fruit.

"Excuse me," she began, trying to sound casual. "I couldn't help but notice there didn't seem to be many children around. Where are they?"

The women exchanged glances, and for a moment, there was an uncomfortable silence.

Finally, one of them, a woman with kind eyes and a wrinkled face, spoke up.

"Most of the young ones have left," she said. "Gone to the city for better opportunities. The few that are left, well, they stay inside mostly."

The younger woman seated beside her added. "Not much for them to do here. No schools, no playgrounds. It's easier to keep them indoors."

"As our children have moved to bigger cities with their own families, the village has no reason to maintain the school and children's facilities anymore."

She added, "It's hard to let go, but the truth is, the vibrant energy that once filled these places with life has shifted elsewhere. Our village has changed, and it feels like we're saying goodbye to a part of our soul."

Zarinah continued her walk, her heart weighed down with a heavy sadness. The absence of children gave the village an eerie, ghost-town-like atmosphere.

It was as if an entire generation had been erased. She found herself at the edge of the village, where the dense jungle began. There, she spotted a small, rundown building. Curiosity piqued; she made her way over.

The building turned out to be an old, abandoned schoolhouse. Its paint was peeling, and the windows were broken. Weeds had overtaken the playground, and the swings hung motionless, creaking eerily in the wind.

Zarinah pushed open the door, and it creaked loudly in protest. Inside, the classroom was dusty and filled with cobwebs, with rocks scattered across the floor. Yet, the desks and blackboard still stood in place.

She imagined the room once filled with children, their laughter echoing off the walls. Now, it stood as a silent testament to a bygone era. As she stood there, she felt a wave of melancholy wash over her.

"What had happened to this village? Why had it been forgotten?"

A sudden faint creak echoed through the dusty, rotting floors to her left, sending a chill down her spine. She turned swiftly, heart pounding, and caught a fleeting glimpse of a shadow, a cat's silhouette, or just the tail end of one.

Her eyes remained fixed on the spot, straining against the darkness, but the figure did not reappear, nor did the eerie silence break. The air was thick with unspoken tension as if the very walls were holding their breath, waiting.

Leaving the old school building, Zarinah knew she had stumbled upon the real story of the village. The school, with its abandoned halls and lingering shadows, held secrets that the present dared not disturb.

The village's story wasn't in the mundane daily routines but in the echoes of its past and the whispers of its future. It wasn't just about the people who remained, but about those who had left and the silence they left behind.

Returning to Kak Wan's store, Zarinah found the elderly woman sitting on her porch, a distant look in her eyes.

"I found the old school," Zarinah said, sitting beside her, her voice barely above a whisper.

Kak Wan nodded, her expression unreadable. "That school used to be full of life," she said softly, her voice tinged with a haunting nostalgia.

She paused, her gaze drifting to the empty playground and the silent classrooms, each a silent testament to days gone by.

"I remember when this place was a beacon of hope," she continued, her voice taking on a wistful tone.

"Children would flood in each morning, their laughter echoing through the halls like music. Their voices were like the heartbeat of this community, giving it life and purpose."

"The school was more than just a place for learning; it was where dreams were nurtured and where families found their strength."

Kak Wan's eyes softened as she recalled the faces of the children she had watched grow up.

"Every child who walked through those doors was a promise of tomorrow. They were the reason parents worked hard and held on to hope, even when times were tough. Their joy and curiosity breathed life into the neighborhood, turning the mundane into something magical."

She smiled faintly, though a trace of sadness lingered in her eyes.

"Those moments created bonds, not just between parents and kids, but among the families themselves."

"The school was a place where everyone came together, where they found a common purpose and a shared sense of belonging."

Kak Wan sighed, her voice growing quieter. "But life has a way of moving on, doesn't it?"

The air grew heavier as if the very spirits of the past were gathering around them. Zarinah sensed that the abandoned school was more than just a relic of a bygone era; it was a portal to the village's deepest, darkest secrets.

She could feel the weight of untold stories pressing down on her, urging her to uncover the truth that lay hidden within the village. And perhaps the elusive, mysterious cat lurking in the shadows.

any given saturdays

IT was the second round of reading the text message. This was exactly why he hated mobile phones. The screen was just too small for his failing eyesight. Reevan squinted at the screen, his thumb hovering over the keypad.

"Join me at Kampung Ketiak?" Zarinah's message read.

Reevan sighed, setting the phone down. It wasn't that he didn't want to help, but the request seemed odd. What on earth was there?

He picked up the phone again, his fingers typing out a response. "Why there? What's so special about it?"

He waited, the seconds ticking by slowly until his phone buzzed with a reply.

Zarinah's message read, "There's something you need to see. Trust me, it's important. Plus, I could use your company."

Reevan frowned. Important? What could be important in a remote village? But then again, what else did he have to do?

It had been ten years since his wife died from colon cancer. It's been over five years since his only son, Karvin, moved to Singapore for work. They hardly meet or speak anymore. His days were a blur of routines and memories.

"Give me one good reason why I should go."

"Because you need this, Reevan. You're stuck in a rut. This village might change that. If you don't feel different after the trip, I'll owe you one."

Reevan hesitated. Zarinah had always been cryptic, but she may be right. What harm could a short trip do?

He thought back to his coaching approach, the way he used to inspire his players to embrace the unexpected. Perhaps it was time to take his own advice.

Reevan glanced skeptically at the phone. "Alright, I'm in. But if this turns out to be some wild goose chase..."

Zarinah replied to him with a reassuring emoji. "It won't be. Pack light. See you tomorrow morning at 8."

Reevan chuckled, shaking his head. But maybe she was right. Maybe he did need this.

The next morning, Reevan packed a small bag and made his way to the meeting point. Zarinah was waiting, a mischievous glint in her eyes.

"Ready for an adventure, old man?" she teased.

Reevan smirked. "Lead the way, young lady."

The drive to Kampung Ketiak was long and winding, taking them through dense forests and narrow mountain roads. Reevan gazed out the window, lost in thought. He had spent so many years coaching young minds, shaping them into better versions of themselves. Yet here he was, feeling more lost than ever.

When they finally arrived, the village was picturesque, seemingly untouched by time. The air was fresh, the sounds of nature a stark contrast to the city noise he was used to. Zarinah led him to an old, dilapidated football field at the edge of the village.

"This is it," she said.

Reevan looked around, confused. "An old football field?"

Zarinah nodded. "This village has a story, Reevan. A story that might just help you find your way again."

As they explored the village, Reevan began to piece together the tale of Kampung Ketiak. It was once a thriving community with a passion for football, much like the teams he used to coach. But over the years, the village had fallen into disrepair, its spirit broken by a series of unfortunate events.

Reevan felt a strange connection to the place. The more he learned about its history, the more he saw parallels to his own life. The village's resilience and its determination to stay relevant sparked something within him.

That morning, as the sun rose over the hills, Reevan sat by the old, abandoned football field, deep in thought. Zarinah joined him, a knowing smile on her face.

"Feeling any different?" she asked.

Reevan nodded slowly. Zarinah patted his shoulder. "Sometimes, you have to lose yourself to find yourself again."

Reevan looked out at the field, a sense of purpose stirring within him. Perhaps this trip wasn't just about the village. It was about rediscovering the fire he once had, the passion for helping others find their path.

The coach looked around him, the place seemed to have slipped through the cracks of modernity. The sight of the once-grand field, now overrun with wild grass and tangled vines, struck a chord in him. The goalposts were rusted and the lines on the field were no longer visible.

Reevan stepped onto the field, his heart heavy with memories of the countless matches he had coached. This field was the pride of the village. Every Saturday, neighboring villages would come here to play. It was like a festival.

He could almost hear the cheers of the crowd, the shouts of the players, the excitement in the air.

"What happened?" he asked softly.

Kak Wan had earlier told Zarinah. "People left. The younger generation moved to the cities for better opportunities."

They sat on the edge of the field, the sun now climbing above them. The quiet beauty of the place, combined with its poignant history, brought a sense of peace and reflection.

Their next stop was the deserted school. The building, though crumbling and overgrown with vines, still held an air of dignity. As they walked through the empty hallways, echoes of laughter and learning seemed to reverberate through the cracked walls.

Zarinah, always searching for a story that would reignite her passion for journalism, felt a pang of sorrow as she looked at the faded drawings on the walls and the broken desks.

"This place used to be full of life," she murmured, her voice tinged with bitterness.

Reevan nodded, his eyes softening with nostalgia. "Schools like this are the heart of a community. It's sad to see it like this."

They ventured into a classroom, the silence pressing down on them. Zarinah picked up a dusty book from the floor, flipping through its yellowed pages.

"I wonder what changed here," she said, more to herself than to Reevan.

"Life happens," Reevan replied quietly. "Communities change, people move on. Sometimes, it feels like the world forgets these places."

Zarinah felt a surge of anger. "It's not fair. These kids, their dreams... it all just vanished."

Reevan placed a gentle hand on her shoulder. "Maybe it's not about what's lost, but what we can do to remember and honor it."

Zarinah broke the silence. "I came here looking for a story, something to reignite my passion for journalism. But all I feel is anger and sadness."

Reevan looked at her, his expression thoughtful. "Maybe that's the story, Zarinah. The emotions, the history, the memories... they all have a story to tell. And maybe, by telling it, you can give this village a voice again."

Zarinah stared back at him, tears welling up in her eyes. "I never thought of it that way. I've been so focused on finding something big, something sensational, that I forgot about the power of the simple, heartfelt stories."

As a consummate journalist, she had always been driven by the pursuit of earth-shattering news and sinister plots. Her career had shaped her to be skeptical and wary, often assuming the worst about people's intentions.

The darker, more dramatic stories were her bread and butter, and she prided herself on uncovering hidden truths and exposing hidden agendas.

But in her relentless quest for the next big scoop, Zarinah had lost sight of the quieter, more profound narratives that existed in the everyday lives of ordinary people.

She had neglected the daily struggles of the man on the street, the small victories and defeats that shaped their lives. The simplicity and authenticity of these personal stories had been overshadowed by her obsession with grandiose and sensationalist headlines.

Now, as she reflected on it, she realized how much she had missed by dismissing these simple, heartfelt stories. The impact of the mundane yet meaningful experiences of everyday people had eluded her, overshadowed by her focus on the dramatic and the extraordinary.

Reevan smiled gently. "Sometimes, it's the small stories that have the biggest impact. This village may be forgotten by the world, but its legacy can live on through your words."

They sat in silence, each lost in their thoughts. As the light began to fade in the evening sky, Zarinah and Reevan left the village with a sense of purpose.

Perhaps they still had something to offer, a way to inspire others through what they do best: coaching and inspiring the next generation.

puss in the woods

AIDEN adjusted the strap of his camera and followed the cat, her shiny black fur almost luminescent against the contrasting green undergrowth. It was as if this mysterious feline were leading him on a guided tour of a world he barely knew existed.

The cat's movements were silent and fluid, effortlessly navigating the dense foliage. She had appeared a short while after Aiden began his walk in the deeper parts of the village.

Every few steps, she glanced back at Aiden, her butter yellow eyes glinting in the dim light that filtered through the canopy. Each time she did, Aiden felt a strange sense of reassurance. It was as if she was silently saying, "Trust me."

The further they went into the forest, the more the world around Aiden seemed to transform. The familiar village trails disappeared, replaced by a labyrinth of shadows and whispers. The air grew cooler, and the scent of earth and moss filled his nostrils.

Suddenly, the cat paused, her ears twitching. Aiden stopped too, holding his breath. He listened, straining to catch the faint sound that had alerted the cat.

After a moment, he heard it, a soft rustling, like leaves brushing against one another. The cat resumed her pace, and Aiden followed, his heart pounding with anticipation.

They emerged into a small clearing, bathed in dappled sunlight. In the center stood an ancient oak tree, its gnarled branches stretching out like the arms of a wise old sage.

At the base of the tree was a natural spring, the water clear and sparkling as it bubbled up from the ground. Aiden raised his camera, captivated by the beauty before him.

The cat sat down beside the spring, her eyes fixed on him as if to say, "This is it."

He knelt, carefully adjusting the settings on his camera to capture the scene. As he snapped photo after photo, he felt a sense of peace wash over him. For the first time in a long while, he wasn't thinking about social media posts or notifications. He was fully present, immersed in the moment.

Suddenly, there was a flutter of wings. Aiden looked up just in time to see a flash of iridescent blue as a kingfisher darted down to the spring. His heart leaped with excitement, and he quickly focused his lens on the bird. The kingfisher perched on a low branch, its bright plumage shimmering in the sunlight.

Aiden snapped several photos, each one more breathtaking than the last. He couldn't believe his luck. The cat had led him to a hidden gem, a secret sanctuary where wildlife thrived.

As the kingfisher flew off, Aiden lowered his camera and looked at the cat. She was still watching him, her emerald eyes filled with an almost knowing expression. He smiled, feeling a deep sense of gratitude.

"Thank you," he whispered. "I wouldn't have found this place without you."

The cat blinked slowly as if acknowledging his words. Then, with a flick of her tail, she turned and disappeared into the undergrowth, just as quickly as she had appeared before him earlier.

Aiden stayed in the clearing for a while longer, soaking in the tranquility and beauty of the place. For too long, Aiden's life had revolved around the pursuit of social media validation.

Each day was a relentless cycle of capturing moments, editing them to perfection, and posting them online with the hope of garnering more likes, more followers, and more approval from strangers.

The thrill of a new notification, the fleeting high from a surge in likes, had become his primary source of fulfillment. But it was a shallow fulfillment, a temporary balm that quickly wore off, leaving him feeling emptier than before.

In this digital quest for approval, Aiden had lost touch with his real-life friends. The genuine laughter and deep conversations he once shared with them had been replaced by the hollow interactions of online comments and messages.

Social activities had become infrequent, replaced by hours spent alone in front of a screen, meticulously curating a digital persona that felt increasingly distant from who he was.

For a few years now, Aiden had felt lost and alone. The thousands of followers, the countless thumbs-ups, and the endless scrolling through other people's perfect lives did little to alleviate his sense of isolation. They only amplified it.

He was surrounded by virtual acquaintances but had no one to truly connect with, no one who knew the real him behind the filtered images and carefully crafted captions.

Aiden's loneliness was exacerbated as each scroll through curated feeds and perfectly staged photos seemed to underscore a growing chasm between his reality and the idealized lives of others. The more he connected online, the more disconnected he felt.

In between posts, Aiden sought refuge in online games. These virtual worlds offered an escape, a way to forget the gnawing emptiness he felt. But they too were a temporary fix, a distraction that only deepened his sense of detachment from the real world.

His relationships were superficial at best, with no steady girlfriend and no meaningful romantic connections.

His only enduring passion was photography, but even that had been reduced to an exercise in envy as he scrolled through the work of professional photojournalists, longing to capture images with the same skill and impact.

At a photography exhibition last year, Aiden found himself face-to-face with the renowned lifestyle photographer, Clara Teoh. The exhibit showcased her striking portraits and captivating street scenes.

Aiden approached Clara; his admiration evident. "Ms. Teoh, your work is incredible. The way you capture people's lives, it's so powerful."

"How do you approach your photography?"

Clara smiled warmly, her eyes twinkling with passion. "Thank you, Aiden. For me, photography isn't just about taking pictures."

"It's about connecting with people on a deeper level. I believe that every face tells a story, and my job is to listen to that story and translate it into an image."

Aiden nodded, intrigued. "That's fascinating. But how do you deal with the challenges of capturing genuine moments?"

Clara's expression softened, and she leaned in slightly. "What I've learned over the years is that the essence of great photography lies in authenticity and empathy."

"It's about finding your voice and perspective. The most impactful images come from truly engaging with your subjects and understanding their stories."

Aiden listened intently, "So, it's about more than just technical skill?"

"Absolutely. Technical skill is important, but it's the emotional connection and the ability to convey a story," she affirmed.

"When you focus on the people and their experiences rather than just the perfect shot, your work becomes more meaningful."

Aiden often found himself wondering when and why he had stopped dreaming. As a child, he had been full of ambition and wonder, eager to explore the world and create something meaningful. But somewhere along the way, that spark had dimmed.

The pressure to conform, to achieve success as defined by social media metrics, had overshadowed his true passions. He had become a spectator in his own life, watching from the sidelines as others lived out their dreams.

The forest here was a stark contrast to this digital existence. It was real, unfiltered, and demanding of his full attention. For a long time, he had been chasing after the perfect shot, the perfect subject, and the perfect angle. But in that serene moment, he realized something profound.

He had been so focused on the pursuit of the ideal image that he had missed the true essence of living in the moment. The beauty he sought was not just in capturing a fleeting second but in fully experiencing it.

The way the sunlight danced across the leaves, the gentle rustling of the branches, and the soft, earthy smell of the forest floor, were the real treasures, the genuine experiences that made life rich and meaningful.

Aiden began to understand that the purpose of photography, and life itself, was not merely to document the extraordinary but to appreciate and immerse oneself in the ordinary. Each moment held its unique beauty, its own story, and it was through embracing these moments that he could truly connect with the world around him.

The sound of birdsong, the feel of the earth beneath his feet, the beauty of a sunbeam piercing through the canopy; these were experiences that couldn't be captured in a photo or distilled into a status update. They were moments to be lived, not just documented.

The encounter with the cat was a turning point. As he followed the cat deeper into the woods, it reminded Aiden of the wonder and curiosity he had once felt as a child. It reignited his passion for exploration and discovery, not just through a lens, but with all his senses.

In the silence of the forest, away from the constant barrage of notifications and the pressure to perform, he found a sense of peace and purpose.

As he walked back to the village, Aiden knew that he needed to make a change. It was time to reconnect with his real-life friends, to engage in social activities that brought genuine joy, and to pursue photography not for the likes and followers, but for the love of capturing the beauty of the world.

When he finally decided to head back, he realized that throughout his exploration in the woods, he hadn't felt the urge to check his phone or rush back to the hustle and bustle of daily life even once. There was something about this newfound peace that resonated deep within him, a tranquil sanctuary for his restless soul.

As he retraced his steps through the forest, Aiden felt a renewed sense of purpose. He knew that he would return soon, not just to capture more photographs, but to reconnect with the simple, profound joy of being in nature.

"But I need something to accompany the photography," Aiden mused.

"If only there were thrilling stories to go with these images. People like captivating narratives and tales that weave breathtaking visuals with compelling stories, keeping viewers hooked."

"That's what I want for my photography; to not just show the beauty of wildlife but to tell the exciting stories behind each shot," he said to himself.

sleepy but not hollow

"HEY, you were there!" Zarinah exclaimed, her voice reverberating through the phone with a mix of excitement and surprise.

She was scrolling through Instagram, her eyes glued to Aiden's latest reel on the wildlife in Kampung Ketiak.

"Coach Reevan and I were just there a few weeks ago," she continued, her voice tinged with an infectious enthusiasm that made Aiden smile on the other end.

By now, Zarinah was deeply engrossed in writing a news story about the village she had accidentally stumbled upon. Her project aimed to capture the essence of life, the echoes of lost memories, and the flickering hope that still burned within the villagers.

"Aiden, I need you to come along," she urged.

"Your photos are exactly what I need to bring the villagers' stories to life. You have a way of capturing emotions, the kind that words alone can't convey."

Aiden hesitated, the weight of his doubts pressing down on him. His passion for wildlife photography was a beacon in his otherwise monotonous life, yet he often felt uncertain about venturing beyond the familiar. But Zarinah's words tugged at something deep within him, a sense of purpose he hadn't felt in a long time.

"Besides," Zarinah added with a playful lilt, "think of all the nature shots you'll get. And the villagers! They have stories that need to be told."

Aiden took a deep breath. "Alright, I'm in. When do we start?"

As they planned their trip, Reevan joined the call with an idea that sparked a renewed sense of hope. "We should rebuild the old football pitch in the village," he suggested.

"It's been abandoned for years, but I think we can bring it back to life. It could be a place for the youth from surrounding villages to come together and play."

The journey to the village was filled with anticipation. The community, with its dense rainforest and vibrant wildlife, was a photographer's paradise. But what struck Aiden most were the people. They carried stories etched in their faces, tales of hardship, resilience, and undying hope.

Zarinah's interviews delved into the villagers' pasts. Her first interview was with Pak Ahmad, the village elder, who recounted the days when Kampung Ketiak was a bustling community.

"We had a thriving market, a school filled with children's laughter, and the football pitch was our pride," he reminisced, his eyes glistening with tears.

"But things changed," he continued, his voice heavy with sorrow. "Natural disasters, economic struggles, and the younger generation leaving for the city left us with empty homes and forgotten dreams."

Aiden's camera clicked, capturing the raw emotion on Pak Ahmad's face. He moved silently, his lens finding moments of vulnerability and strength in equal measure.

The next person to step in front of Zarinah was Pak Wahab, the comical chicken-only restaurant operator. Known for his infectious laughter and endless jokes, he was the town jester. As he settled into the interview chair, a mischievous grin spread across his face.

"So, Pak Wahab, tell us about the village in its heyday," Zarinah prompted, already anticipating a lively conversation.

"Ah, the 70s!" Pak Wahab exclaimed, his eyes twinkling. "Back then, this village was like a hive of activity, buzzing louder than a beehive stuck in a drum!" He chuckled, pausing to let his laughter fill the room.

"We were famous for our flowers and tropical fruits," he continued, his voice brimming with pride.

"People would come from all over just to buy our orchids. They were so beautiful that even the bees would get confused and start romancing them!"

Everyone laughed, including Aiden, who was busy capturing the lively expressions on Pak Wahab's face.

"And the fruits! Oh, the fruits!" Pak Wahab said, widening his eyes dramatically.

"We had durians so delicious; they could make a grown man cry. Of course, the smell could also make a grown man cry, but that's a different story." He winked, and the shop erupted in laughter again.

"The village was nestled in a valley with fertile grounds," Pak Wahab explained, his tone becoming more nostalgic.

"Everything we planted flourished. It was like the soil itself was blessed. We had rambutan, mangosteen, and pineapples. I used to say that our fruits are so good, even the monkeys pay us!"

Zarinah smiled warmly, appreciating the humor laced with a genuine fondness for the village's past.

"But then," Pak Wahab's voice took on a more somber note, "times changed. Nearby townships popped up, offering better pay and easier lifestyles."

"The young ones left for the bigger cities, chasing dreams that couldn't grow in our small village soil."

He paused, the weight of his words settling between us. "As they left, the village began to wither. The vibrant chatter of children, once so familiar, grew faint."

"The elders, my peers, who had spent their lives nurturing this place, now found themselves in a quiet, empty place."

Pak Wahab's eyes grew distant, lost in the memories of days gone by.

"It wasn't just the noise that left. It was the joy, the spirit of daily living. The simple pleasures, morning greetings, shared meals, evening stories by the fire, those things seemed to vanish as well."

He shook his head slowly as if trying to clear the melancholy that had settled over him.

"We felt forgotten, as if the world had moved on and left us behind. The elders, with their stories and wisdom, were left adrift in a sea of change, their contributions and presence rendered almost invisible."

Aiden's camera clicked quietly, capturing the shift in Pak Wahab's expression. The laughter lines around his eyes seemed deeper, etched by years of change and loss.

"The football field used to be our pride and joy," Pak Wahab continued.

"We had football matches every Saturday. Kids would play from dawn till dusk, their shouts and laughter filling the air."

"But as the youths left, the matches stopped, and the field fell silent."

Zarinah nodded, feeling the weight of Pak Wahab's words. The story was not just one of a place but of its people, their joys, their struggles, and their enduring spirit.

"But you know," Pak Wahab said, his grin returning, "we still have the best chicken-only restaurant around. It's so good, even the vegetarians sneak in for a bite!" He laughed, breaking the solemnity with his trademark humor.

finding neemo

WITH the blessing of the village elders, Reevan hired a bulldozer to flatten the football field and clear out the surrounding area. It was a momentous occasion, signaling the start of a new chapter for the villagers.

A week later, Reevan was back, overseeing the replanting of cow grass for the field, his heart filled with a sense of purpose. He was in his element, directing, and guiding the workers.

His enthusiasm was contagious, and soon the village buzzed with anticipation. He even found a sponsor willing to fund the building of a simple covered spectator stand and a waist-high iron fence to keep cows and other animals off the pitch.

Amidst all the activity, Reevan noticed a shy girl of about twelve who was always nearby. She didn't speak much, but her presence was constant. She helped with small tasks, like passing Reevan a hammer or pushing the equipment cart.

A silky black cat, her inseparable companion, always followed her.

One afternoon, as Reevan was painting the lines on the field, the girl approached, holding a brush and a can of paint.

"Here, let me help," she said softly, her eyes fixed on the ground.

Reevan smiled warmly. "Thank you. What's your name?"

She hesitated, then replied, "Neemo."

"Nice to meet you, Neemo. That's a beautiful cat you have there," Reevan said, gesturing to the black cat curling around her feet.

"This is Bob," Neemo said, her voice barely above a whisper. "She's my best friend."

Reevan knelt to pet Bob. "Hello. You know, Neemo, I think it's wonderful that you're helping. It's a big job, and every little bit counts."

Neemo's cheeks flushed with a shy smile. "I just want to see the field finished. My grandfather used to tell me stories about the games they played here. I never got to see one."

Reevan's heart ached with the weight of her words. "Well, we're going to make sure you get to see many games here. This field is for you and all the kids in the village."

As the days went by, Reevan and Neemo developed a quiet camaraderie. He learned that she lived with her grandparents and had lost her parents in a tragic accident seven years ago. Bob had been her solace, her constant companion through the tough times.

One evening, as the sun dipped below the horizon, casting a golden glow over the field, Reevan sat on the edge of the half-finished spectator stand, wiping sweat from his brow. Neemo sat beside him, Bob nestled in her lap.

"You know, Neemo, when I was your age, football was my escape," Reevan began, his voice gentle. "It gave me a sense of belonging, a place where I felt I could be myself."

Neemo looked up, her eyes filled with curiosity. "Did you play a lot?"

Reevan chuckled. "Every chance I got. I wasn't the best player, but I loved it. And now, I want to give you and the other children that same feeling."

"This field isn't just grass and lines. It's a place where dreams can grow."

Neemo nodded thoughtfully. "I think my parents would have liked that. They always wanted me to be happy."

Reevan placed a reassuring hand on her shoulder. "And they would be proud of you, Neemo. You're helping to build something special here."

In the following days, the field began to take shape. The grass grew lush and green, the spectator stand stood tall, and the iron fence was firmly in place. The village buzzed with excitement, anticipation hanging in the air.

On the day of the grand reopening, the entire village gathered around the newly restored football field. The elders gave their blessings, and Reevan stood proudly with Neemo and Bob by her side.

As the first game between the villagers and guests from nearby estates began, Neemo's eyes sparkled with joy. The shouts and laughter of the villagers filled the air, bringing life back to the village.

Reevan watched with a heart full of pride, knowing that together, they had rebuilt more than just a field. They had rebuilt hope and dreams.

Neemo turned to Reevan, a radiant smile on her face. "Thank you, Reevan. For everything."

Reevan smiled back, his eyes glistening. "No, Neemo. Thank you. For reminding me why we do this."

the vanishing

ZARINAH'S heart pounded in her chest as she read Aiden's message again, hoping she had misunderstood. But the words remained the same.

"They are calling you a fraud!"

Just two weeks ago, her groundbreaking report on Kampung Ketiak had thrust her into the limelight. The remote village, hidden from modern civilization, had captivated the world with its untouched beauty and unique personalities. Job offers had poured in, and she was relishing her return to prominence in the media industry.

Now, everything was unraveling. Readers claim they had tried to find Kampung Ketiak but discovered no trace of the village. They accused Zarinah of fabricating the entire story. Panic gripped her.

How could this be? She had been there, spoken to the villagers, walked the dusty paths, and watched children play football in the open field.

Determined to clear her name, Zarinah called Aiden. "We need to go back," she said, her voice trembling with urgency.

"We need to prove them wrong."

Aiden agreed without hesitation. He had been her closest ally throughout the adventure.

Three days later, they drove to the remote region where Kampung Ketiak was supposed to be. As they approached the location, Zarinah's anxiety grew. She had expected to see the familiar sight of wooden houses and the bustling village square. Instead, there was nothing but dense forest.

They parked the car where the ever-present Kak Wan always waited outside her shop, half expecting her to appear and clear up the confusion. She did not.

They ventured into the woods on foot, the path they had walked just weeks before was overgrown and unrecognizable. The village, the shops, the field, everything was gone. Not a single trace remained.

Zarinah's mind raced. How could an entire village vanish? Desperation clawed at her as they searched for any sign of life. But there was nothing. They called out for the villagers they had met, for the children who had laughed and played, for Pak Wahab who had shared his stories. Silence was their only answer.

"Where is everyone?" Aiden asked, his voice tinged with disbelief.

Zarinah shook her head, feeling a sinking dread. "I don't know," she whispered. "But we need to find out."

They tried calling Coach Reevan, but there was no response. He had gone silent, just as the accusations against Zarinah had started to surface. It was as if he had vanished along with the village.

As the sun began to set, casting long shadows through the trees, Zarinah and Aiden returned to their car, their minds heavy with unanswered questions. They decided to visit the nearest town, hoping to find someone who might have seen or heard something.

At the town's small coffee shop, they struck up a conversation with the owner, an elderly man who had lived in the area his entire life. When they mentioned Kampung Ketiak, he gave them a puzzled look.

"Kampung Ketiak?" he said, his voice tinged with surprise. "Wow, I haven't heard that name in years!"

Zarinah and Aiden exchanged a confused glance. "What do you mean?" Zarinah asked. "We were just there last month."

The man shook his head. "Kampung Ketiak was abandoned over fifty years ago. The villagers left, and the jungle reclaimed the land."

Zarinah felt a chill run down her spine. "But that's impossible. We saw the village. We spoke to the people."

The man regarded them with a mix of curiosity and concern. "Sometimes, the past has a way of reaching out to us," he said cryptically.

"Perhaps what you saw was a glimpse of what once was."

Zarinah and Aiden left the café in a daze, their minds reeling. Had they somehow stepped into a fragment of history? Had the village been a mirage, a momentary glimpse into a forgotten past?

As they drove back to the city, a heavy silence filled the car. Zarinah's thoughts raced, trying to make sense of everything. The elderly man's words echoed in her mind. Had they experienced a fragment of history?

She glanced at Aiden, who was equally lost in thought.

"What if this was all a dream? What if we never really went there?"

Aiden shook his head slowly. "It felt real, Zarinah. We have photos, notes, and interviews, and we even rebuilt a whole football field. It wasn't just a dream."

"But how do we explain what happened?" Zarinah asked, frustration creeping into her voice.

"How does a village disappear without a trace?"

Aiden sighed. "I don't know. But we need to figure it out."

Back in the city, Zarinah pored over her notes and photos, looking for any clue that might explain the mystery. She noticed something strange. The photos of the villagers and the village itself had a hazy, almost surreal quality to them. It was as if they were looking at images from another time.

Determined to get to the bottom of this, Zarinah contacted a professor of local history at a nearby university. Dr. Rajesh was intrigued by her story and agreed to meet her.

In his cluttered office, Dr. Rajesh examined the photos and listened intently to Zarinah's account.

"There have been stories," he said slowly, "of places that exist outside of time. Places that appear for a moment and then vanish. These stories are often dismissed as folklore or hallucinations."

"But we were there," Zarinah insisted. "It was real."

Dr. Rajesh nodded. "I'm not saying it wasn't. But perhaps you experienced something beyond our understanding of reality. There are many mysteries in this world, things that cannot be explained by science alone."

With renewed determination, Zarinah and Aiden set out to uncover the secrets of Kampung Ketiak. They visited local libraries, searched through old records, and interviewed anyone who might have information about the village.

One evening, as they were going through a dusty archive in the city's oldest library, Zarinah stumbled upon a faded journal. The journal belonged to a man named Malik, who had lived in the village.

Flipping through the pages, Zarinah read about the village's struggle to survive in the face of modernization. Malik wrote about the villagers' decision to leave and their hope that one day, someone would remember them and tell their story.

lost – the sequel

"WELL, this is a fine mess," Aiden muttered, scratching his head.

"One minute I was finally happy doing what I wanted, and the next, it's all gone like a puff of smoke."

His friend Jack, ever the pragmatist, quickly took stock of their situation. "You need to figure out what happened. There must be some clues left behind."

Aiden reached into his bag pack and took out a curious item; a small, intricately carved, palm-sized wooden box he found half-buried in the dirt when he and Zarinah were there a couple of days back. He opened it to reveal a cryptic note.

The note read, "To find what is lost, follow the trail of one that stays in the shadows and never speaks."

Jack asked, raising an eyebrow. "What on earth does that mean?"

The air hung heavy with the silence of an empty canvas. The young men were now back at the site of the vanished village where vibrant life had pulsed months ago. Aiden traced the outline of the village elder's hut, now nothing more than a ghostly impression on the ground. Vanished. Like a dream fading at dawn.

Aiden and Jack stood there, a pair of disheartened figures against the backdrop of a village that seemed to have been erased by some ethereal hand. The silence was thick and oppressive, only broken by the occasional rustle of the leaves as a breeze drifted by, carrying with it the faintest whisper of secrets long buried.

"Well, if that isn't the queerest thing," Jack muttered, squinting at the note as if willing it to reveal its mysteries.

"A trail of shadows and silence. Reminds me of my mum's cooking, invisible and not a peep of flavor."

Aiden gave a half-hearted chuckle, his mind racing through the possibilities.

"It's like something out of those old stories. You know, the ones where the hero must solve riddles and follow clues left by some ancient, all-knowing oracle."

Jack scratched his chin thoughtfully. "Yeah, well, I don't recall any of those stories ending well for the hero, or his sidekick."

"Trouble or not, we don't have much of a choice," Aiden said, his resolve hardening. "We've got to follow the clue."

They set off, moving cautiously through the remnants of the village. The path was faint, barely more than a whisper in the dust, but it was there if you knew how to look. Aiden's eyes darted to the shadows, trying to catch a glimpse of the elusive figure the note spoke of.

Their journey led them to the edge of the village and into the forest beyond. The trees stood tall and silent, like ancient sentinels guarding secrets older than time. The deeper they went, the darker it grew, until the sunlight was little more than a memory, replaced by the cool embrace of the forest shadows.

"I feel like we're being watched," Jack whispered.

"Constantly," Aiden added, his eyes scanning the darkness. He could feel it too, that prickling sensation on the back of his neck, like a pair of eyes following their every move.

They reached a clearing where the trees parted to reveal an ancient, crumbling stone archway. Vines and moss clung to its weathered surface, and an eerie silence filled the air. Aiden approached cautiously, his hand resting on the hilt of his dad's parang.

As they passed through the archway, the temperature seemed to drop, and a thick fog rolled in, swirling around their ankles. Ahead, barely visible in the gloom, was a figure cloaked in shadow, standing perfectly still.

"That must be it," Aiden whispered, his heart pounding in his chest. "The one that stays in the shadows and never speaks."

They stepped forward. The figure remained silent, unmoving. They realized it was merely a tree stump with a weathered drooping branch at its side pointing towards a faded clearing to the right.

"Not sure if that's the answer to the clue, but it is a lead," Jack said, his voice trembling slightly. With a nod, Aiden led the way, following the path indicated by the silent figure.

The forest seemed to close in around them, the shadows growing darker and more oppressive. Yet there was a strange sense of purpose, a feeling that they were on the right track, even if the destination remained shrouded in mystery.

`They walked for hours; the only sounds were the crunch of leaves underfoot and the occasional snap of a twig. Just when they began to wonder if they were lost, the path opened into another clearing.

Jack spotted the silhouette of a cat about ten feet ahead of the new path. As they walked towards it, Aiden exclaimed: "That's Bob!"

Aiden had met Bob, the village cat, during his previous visit. She seemed confident enough with her new acquaintances to merge from behind the trees, its eyes glowing like twin lanterns in the ghostly light.

Bob's sleek black fur absorbed the ethereal glow, making the cat look like a living shadow.

It moved with an eerie grace, weaving between Aiden and Jack before settling in front of them, its gaze locked onto Aiden's.

"Well, I'll be," Aiden whispered, his voice barely audible. "That cat's got more lives than a politician's promises."

He knelt, extending his hand cautiously. "Well, you stay in the shadows, never speak, and you sure know your way around."

Bob blinked slowly, then turned and began to walk toward the far side of the clearing, glancing back to ensure they were following. Aiden and Jack exchanged a glance before stepping after the cat, their footsteps muffled by the soft earth.

The path Bob led them on was narrow and winding, bordered by ancient trees whose gnarled branches twisted and turned like the fingers of forgotten giants. The air was thick with the scent of moss and damp earth, and the occasional hoot of an owl echoed through the forest.

After what felt like an eternity, they arrived at a small, secluded glade. In the center stood an old stone well, its surface covered in intricate carvings that seemed to dance in the faint light. Bob circled the well once before sitting down, curling its tail around its paws.

"This place gives me the creeps," Jack muttered, shivering despite himself.

"Feels like we're in the heart of some ancient secret."

Aiden approached the well, his curiosity piqued. "There's something here, Jack. I can feel it." He peered into the well, but the darkness inside seemed impenetrable.

"What do you think is down there?" Jack asked, glancing nervously at the well.

"Only one way to find out," Aiden replied as he took a climbing rope from his bag and secured it tightly to a sturdy tree branch nearby before lowering it into the well.

"I'll go first. Keep an eye on things up here."

Jack nodded, gripping the rope tightly as Aiden began his descent. The cool, damp walls of the well seemed to close in around him, and the darkness grew thicker with every step. Finally, his feet touched solid ground.

"Aiden?" Jack's voice echoed faintly from above.

"I'm okay," Aiden called back. "I think I see something."

He reached into his pocket and pulled out a small flashlight, flicking it on. The beam cut through the darkness, revealing an underground chamber. The walls were lined with ancient carvings, like those on the well's surface, and in the center of the chamber lay a stone pedestal. Atop it rested a small, ornate chest, its surface gleaming in the flashlight's beam.

Aiden approached the chest cautiously, his heart pounding in his chest. He reached out, his fingers brushing against the cold metal. The lid creaked open, revealing a trove of faded letters.

He picked up a handful of the letters. Although worn with age, they were still legible. They were folded and without envelopes. As Aiden flipped through them, he felt a connection, as if the letters were a key to understanding the mysteries that had led them here.

"Aiden, what did you find?" Jack's voice brought him back to the present. Aiden climbed the rope, emerging from the well with a sense of triumph. Jack and Bob watched him expectantly.

Jack, with a furrowed brow, held up one of the letters, its edges curling with age. "How did these letters end up here?"

"What happened to the people who wrote these? Did they leave the village, as so many others did? Or did they somehow become part of this place; their stories buried just like these letters?"

The letters seemed to whisper their tales, their ink smudged by time and water. As Aiden and Jack pondered these questions, they began to realize that uncovering the stories behind these letters might reveal more about the village's lost history and the people who once lived there.

Their search for answers was just beginning, and each letter held the promise of untold stories, leading them deeper into the mysteries of the village and its past.

letters to julie

AIDEN sat in the dimly lit storeroom, long forgotten in his family's bungalow. The air was thick with the scent of aged paper and wood, decades have passed since anyone had ventured into this neglected corner of the house.

Here, undisturbed, he intended to dip into the sea of correspondence, just skimming the surface of what seemed an endless repository of over a hundred letters.

They were bound together with a fraying ribbon, the paper yellowed and brittle with age. Each letter was meticulously handwritten, the ink faded but still readable.

As he untied the ribbon and began to read, he was transported to a different time, a different world.

The first letter was from a father to his children. The handwriting was neat but carried the weight of a heavy heart. The father wrote about the struggles of their village, a place that seemed unable to move on with the times.

He spoke of the old ways, the traditions that had defined their community for generations, and his fear that these would be lost as the world changed around them.

"My dearest children," the letter began, "I write to you with a heart full of sorrow and a mind clouded by the uncertainty of our future."

"Our village, once thriving with the laughter and hard work of our people, now stands at a crossroads."

"The world beyond our hills beckons with promises of progress and prosperity, yet I fear the cost of such advancement. Will we, in our pursuit of a better life, lose the very essence of who we are?"

Aiden could almost hear the old man's voice, quivering with emotion, as he expressed his fears of being left behind, of watching his children leave for a better future while he remained rooted in the past.

The next letter was from a mother, lamenting the growing distance between her and her daughter. Her words were tinged with a deep sadness, a sense of abandonment. She wrote about how her child, once so close and attentive, had become a stranger, her life consumed by the demands of the modern world.

"My beloved Julie," she wrote, "I fear I am but a ghost in your life now. You rush through your days, consumed by the ceaseless march of time, and I am left behind in the stillness of our home."

"Do you remember the stories I used to tell you, the songs we sang together? Or have those memories faded as swiftly as the seasons change? I long for the days when we were together, truly together, not just in body but in spirit."

Aiden felt a pang of empathy for the mother, imagining her sitting alone in a quiet house, surrounded by echoes of the past.

The third letter was the most heart-wrenching. It was from a father who confessed his hesitation to allow his children to be educated. He feared that education would lead them away from the village, away from him.

His struggle was evident in every word, a battle between his desire for their betterment and his fear of being left behind.

"To my dear children," he penned, "I know that the world beyond our village offers you opportunities that I never had. Education is a gift, a pathway to a brighter future."

"Yet, I am plagued by a selfish fear. What if, in seeking knowledge and prosperity, you find yourselves drifting away from me, from our home?"

"I have always wished for your happiness, but I cannot bear the thought of being left alone, forgotten."

Tears welled up in Aiden's eyes as he imagined the father's inner turmoil, his love for his children clashing with his fear of solitude.

The final letter he read was a suicide note, written by a young woman overwhelmed by anger and despair. Her words were raw, unfiltered, a cry of anguish against the injustices of life and the grip of poverty.

She spoke of her dreams, crushed under the weight of circumstances, and her decision to escape a life that had offered her nothing but pain.

"To whoever finds this," she began, "I am weary of this life, of the endless struggle against a world that seems determined to break me. Poverty has been my constant companion, robbing me of hope, of joy."

"I have fought for so long, but I can no longer bear the weight. I leave this world not in defeat, but in defiance, refusing to let it strip me of my last shred of dignity."

The raw emotion in her words left Aiden shaken. He could feel her anger, her despair, her sense of hopelessness. As he carefully folded the letters and placed them back in the bundle, he realized these were just a fraction of the vast number of letters still waiting to be read.

He realized that despite their differences, each letter shared a common thread: regret.

Each writer was penning their final words, their last attempt to make sense of their lives and the choices they had made.

The father regretted not embracing change sooner, the mother regretted the growing distance from her daughter, the other father regretted his fear of losing his children to education, and the young woman regretted a life of unfulfilled dreams.

Aiden sat in the room for a long time, the letters resting in his lap. These were not just letters; they were the voices of the villagers' ancestors, their fears, hopes, and regrets etched into paper.

The letters had given him a glimpse into the lives of those who had come before him, their struggles, and sacrifices. Stories that must be told.

With the letters all carefully put away into a plastic storage box, he pondered. "Who will be able to turn these letters into stories that will capture the world's attention?"

pursuit of happiness

COACH Reevan stood in the living room, staring at the worn photo of his late wife. Her eyes seemed to bore into him, reminding him of all he had failed to be, a compassionate husband and an understanding father. The emptiness of the house echoed his guilt, a constant reminder of the harsh words exchanged with his son, Karvin.

Karvin burst through the front door; his face flushed with anger. "Why can't you ever understand me, Dad?"

"Why do you always have to control everything I do?"

Reevan's voice was cold and stern, masking the turmoil inside. "Because I'm your father, and I know what's best for you! This world isn't as forgiving as you think."

Karvin's eyes glistened with unshed tears. "You don't know anything about me! You never listen!"

"Ever since Mom died, you've been impossible to talk to."

Reevan's face hardened. "Don't you dare bring your mother into this! She would've wanted you to be strong, not run away from your responsibilities."

Karvin's voice broke. "All I wanted was for you to be there for me, Dad. To understand what I'm going through."

"But you were too busy being the 'strong' parent to notice that I needed you."

The silence that followed was deafening, each man's unspoken words hanging heavy in the air. The rift between them grew wider, an abyss filled with regret and missed opportunities.

Missed opportunities best describe Aiden's young life. As he sat by his grandmother's bedside, the steady beep of the heart monitor was a painful reminder of her frailty. Her once vibrant eyes were now dull, clouded by the pain of her illness. Yet, her grip on his hand was as firm as ever.

"Grandma, I'm so lost," Aiden whispered, tears streaming down his face.

"I don't know what to do with my life. I feel trapped in Dad's business, but I don't dare to leave."

Her voice was weak but filled with warmth. "Aiden, my dear, life is too short to live with regrets. You must follow your heart. Be brave and be true to yourself."

"But what if I fail?" Aiden's voice trembled.

She smiled faintly, squeezing his hand. "Failure is just a part of life. It's how you grow. Promise me you'll be your own man, Aiden. Promise me you'll chase your dreams, no matter how scary it seems."

Aiden nodded; his heart heavy yet filled with resolve. "I promise, Grandma."

Her eyes closed slowly, a peaceful expression on her face. "That's my boy," she murmured before drifting off to sleep.

It was their last conversation. She lost her three-year battle with cancer just a week later.

Aiden had always found solace in his grandmother's presence. She was the only one who truly understood him, a beacon of unwavering support amidst the turbulence of his family life.

He remembered their conversations fondly, how she would listen with genuine interest as he poured out his heart, unburdening himself of his fears and dreams.

In contrast, his mother seemed perpetually preoccupied with maintaining the perfect image for his celebrated father. She was always by his side, attending social events and mingling with other high-profile figures, leaving Aiden feeling like a mere afterthought.

His mother's preoccupation with her social status left Aiden feeling more isolated than ever, and the absence of his grandmother's empathetic ear only magnified his loneliness.

Empathetic was far from how Zarinah's marriage had been. She stood staring at the emptiness in her closet where Shukri's clothes used to hang, the void a painful reminder of the love and warmth that had slipped through her fingers.

The weight of her regrets pressed heavily on her shoulders. She had always been so focused on her career, her ambition blinding her to the needs of those she loved.

Shukri stood in the doorway, a suitcase in hand. His face was a mask of pain and resignation. "I'm leaving, Zarinah. I can't do this anymore."

Zarinah's voice was desperate. "Shukri, please. Don't go. We can work this out."

Shukri shook his head, tears brimming in his eyes. "I've been patient, Zarinah. I've tried to understand your pressures at work and your ambitions."

"But you've pushed me away for too long. I've always been at the receiving end of your anger, your frustrations. I can't take it anymore."

"You're not leaving because of me," she pleaded. "It's my job, my stress. You know that."

He sighed heavily. "It's not just your job. It's you. You've never seen me as your equal, never valued my love or my support. To you, I'm just the person you come home to, not your partner, not your equal."

Zarinah's voice broke as tears welled in her eyes. "I love you, Shukri. I need you," she whispered, her voice trembling with the weight of unspoken fears.

"I can't do this alone. Our children... they need their father."

Shukri's gaze softened, but his resolve remained. "It's too late now. I need to find my peace, my happiness."

As Shukri walked out the door, the silence that followed was filled with the haunting echoes of her regrets.

city of angels

HE opened his eyes, groggy and unsure of where he was. The room around him was dimly lit, with the smell of burning charcoal hanging in the air. It resembled a wooden shed, but the unfamiliar darkness added to his disorientation.

The football coach looked around for any sign of life but found none. "Where am I?" he murmured; his voice soft against the wooden walls.

Gingerly, Reevan sat up from the bare wooden bed frame, feeling the rough surface against his skin. His legs were cold, and he fumbled for something to cover them. At the foot of the bed, he found a tattered blanket and wrapped it around himself, rising unsteadily to his feet.

The door creaked open, and a figure entered the room. Outside light illuminated a tall man with a weathered face and piercing eyes.

"You're awake," the man said in a deep, calm voice. "How are you feeling?"

Reevan blinked, trying to clear his head. "Confused. Where am I?"

The man approached, his movements deliberate, as though each step carried the weight of years of unseen burdens. His eyes, intense yet compassionate, met Reevan's with a knowing gaze.

"You're in what you have come to know as Kampung Ketiak," he began softly, his voice a mix of reverence and solemnity.

"In truth, there is no name to where we are."

Reevan felt a shiver run down his spine, his mind racing with questions and uncertainty. The man's words hung in the air, resonating with a sense of mystery and profound purpose.

The man, slightly hunched and possibly in his sixties, sighed and settled onto a wooden stool near the bed.

"This place is where people who have lost their purpose in life come to exist," he began, his voice carrying a weight of wisdom.

"Like angels watching over those in the real world, we guide them through loneliness, lost love, emptiness, or grief."

Reevan thought aloud, "It sounds like I am in one of those shows and movies where angels or divine guides explore themes of love, purpose, and redemption." He dared not say it out loud to his host.

"Am I dead?" Reevan asked, his voice tinged with uncertainty.

The man looked at him thoughtfully, the firelight casting shadows across his hardened face. "I won't call it dead," he replied gently, "but rather more like you have become a guardian angel."

Reevan's brow furrowed in confusion. "A guardian angel?"

"Yes," the man continued, his voice calm yet solemn.

"In this place, time flows differently. You're not departed from the world, but rather entrusted with a new purpose; to watch over and guide those who are lost or in need."

Reevan pondered the man's words, the weight of their meaning settling in his mind. 'But why me?' The coach was thinking about the football field he rebuilt and the smiles on the villagers' faces."

The man seemed to know what Reevan was thinking.

"Exactly. Your empathy and understanding will be your greatest tools. You'll listen to their stories, offer comfort, and help them see the path ahead."

Memories of his struggles and triumphs flashed before him. The coach realized that his journey wasn't just about healing others but also finding solace and purpose within himself.

"Will I ever return to my old life?" Reevan asked, his voice tinged with a hint of longing.

The man's gaze softened with understanding. "Perhaps, one day. But for now, your presence here is vital."

"Trust in the journey, Reevan. The answers will come in their own time."

Abruptly, a young girl burst in, accompanied by a black cat. Reevan turned to see the girl, her face lit up with joy at their unexpected reunion.

"Neemo! Bob! What are you both doing here?"

The man smiled warmly. "Neemo and Bob are like you too. They have been with us for a few years now," the man explained warmly, gesturing towards the girl and the black cat.

"They arrived here in much the same way, drawn by a purpose greater than themselves. Neemo, with her boundless curiosity, and Bob, ever watchful and wise, have become integral parts of our community."

He smiled fondly at the pair, whose presence radiated a quiet wisdom and an unspoken bond with the mysterious village.

The coach asked, "What happens after we've helped them?"

The man's gaze softened. "Like you, they move on, guided by newfound strength and purpose. Our mission is to ensure that no one feels lost forever."

Reevan felt a sense of duty and compassion welling within him. "How do I know who needs help?"

"You'll feel it," the man replied gently. "Their pain will resonate with yours, and you'll know."

The man looked at Aiden with a grin, "You know, as a coach, you've always had this knack for pushing people to find their way in sports. Well, guess what? It's the same for life as well."

"Everyone's scared to take new steps or move on, and it's your job to give them a nudge, even if that means being a bit of a tough love guru."

"It's the same game, just a different playing field. And who knows? You might even find that you've got a knack for this whole life-coaching thing after all."

As Reevan absorbed the weight of these revelations, he felt a mixture of awe and apprehension. The enormity of his newfound role as a guardian and guide in this ethereal realm began to dawn on him.

"I know this is overwhelming," the man said gently, his hand resting reassuringly on Reevan's shoulder.

"But trust that you are here for a reason. Your presence in Kampung Ketiak was no accident."

Reevan nodded slowly, his gaze fixed on the horizon beyond the wooden walls of the shed. The weight of responsibility settled upon him, tempered by a sense of purpose that stirred his soul.

As the man turned to leave, Reevan called out, "Wait! I never asked your name?"

The host paused at the doorway, looking back with a faint smile. "I am Malik."

armpit smells like a pulitzer

OVER the next ten months, life for Aiden and Zarinah took a turn that neither could have predicted.

Zarinah, with her characteristic determination and flair for storytelling, transformed Aiden's discovered letters into a national bestseller. The book, aptly titled *Echoes of the Village*, struck a chord with readers across the country.

It was not just a recounting of old letters; it became a journey through time and emotion, weaving together the voices of the past with Zarinah's own experiences and reflections.

"Can you believe it, Aiden?" Zarinah exclaimed over the plate of nasi lemak one evening.

"We've sold out the first print run in a month! And they are translating it into Bahasa Malaysia and Chinese now. This is beyond anything I ever imagined!"

Aiden chuckled on the side of the coffee table, still amazed at how their quiet project had taken on a life of its own.

"I knew those letters were special, but this is something else. People are connecting with the stories."

"I keep thinking about how these letters were almost lost to time," Zarinah mused, sipping her cup of green tea.

"What if they had remained hidden in that well forever?"

Aiden leaned back in his chair, contemplating her words. "It's like we've given them a second life, isn't it?

"And not just their stories," Zarinah added thoughtfully, "but our story too. The story of how two unlikely collaborators unearthed a treasure trove of history and turned it into something meaningful."

Through Zarinah's vivid storytelling and Aiden's adept use of digital platforms, *Echoes of the Village* transcended its pages to become a cultural sensation.

Zarinah, with her innate ability to weave together the threads of tradition and modernity, crafted a narrative that resonated deeply with readers across generations. Her prose painted vibrant landscapes of the village life, capturing not only its picturesque beauty but also the intricate tapestry of human emotions and relationships.

Aiden and his digital media prowess amplified the impact of Zarinah's editorial work. Through strategic social media campaigns, engaging podcasts, and interactive discussions, he brought the book to a global audience hungry for authentic stories.

The novel sparked conversations on cultural identity, the evolving nature of communities, and the timeless themes of love and loss that reverberated through its pages.

"What would Reevan have said about all this?" he wondered aloud, his voice tinged with both nostalgia and a yearning for mentorship. The question hung in the air; a poignant reminder of the void left by the coach's mysterious disappearance.

Amid their success, Aiden and Zarinah continued to honor Reevan's legacy. They dedicated readings and discussions to his memory, celebrating his belief in the power to inspire. Each chapter they penned, each social media post they crafted, was imbued with a sense of gratitude for the coach's tutelage.

The sudden clash of plates behind them jolted them both, making them spin around with reflexive curiosity. The scene that greeted them was one of mild chaos: the waiter, a young man with an apologetic demeanor, was stumbling over his own feet, his face flushed with embarrassment.

He was trying to salvage the situation, mumbling hurried apologies to a man in a baseball cap and a young girl seated at the table.

The man gave a resigned shrug, while the girl's eyes darted around with a mixture of surprise and amusement. The waiter looked like he had slipped on something on the floor, his attempt to clear the plates resulting in a spectacularly noisy disaster.

As the waiter continued to awkwardly gather the fallen silverware, Aiden and Zarinah turned back to their conversation. The incident had momentarily added an unexpected twist to their evening; ironically mirroring the disruptions occurring in their own lives.

As *Echoes of the Village* garnered accolades and touched the hearts of readers worldwide, Aiden found solace in knowing their work had instilled the importance of following one's passion and not living with regret. He remained a part-time photographer, still needing his dad's job to keep his Tesla charged and his dreams afloat.

Zarinah became the darling of her profession once again, but more importantly, she discovered that her storytelling could bring joy to communities and people. It wasn't just about her glory or credentials anymore, though having her kids proudly show off her book to their classmates certainly didn't hurt!

epilogue: dead paw~ets society

AS the sun began its descent, casting a warm, amber glow over the cozy café, a hush of introspection settled in.

The lady in her mid-thirties sighed deeply, her shoulders sagging beneath the invisible weight of the day's frustrations. She stared into her coffee cup as if it held the answers to her discontent.

"Life is increasingly tough. Work is just a daily grind of saying yes to the boss," she grumbled to her colleague, her voice heavy with exhaustion and resignation.

She continued, "I feel like I'm on a hamster wheel, running fast but never getting anywhere. I'm just so tired of the endless cycle."

Her colleague glanced up from his phone and offered a sympathetic nod. He attempted to offer solace. "Maybe it's time to take a step back and ask what makes you happy."

"Sometimes, breaking the cycle means leaping into the unknown."

Meanwhile, at the other end of the café, a young couple was embroiled in their drama. Their voices rose and fell in an emotional duet of frustration and hurt.

The man was exasperated. "We're drowning in bills, and you keep buying things we don't need!"

The woman, with a touch of defiance and a hint of desperation, shot back, "These small luxuries are my way of coping with the stress! If I didn't have these little indulgences, I'd lose my mind!"

Their argument, while intense, was a dance of shared vulnerability. They clashed over finances, yet beneath their harsh words lay an aching desire to understand and support each other.

A few tables to the right, a teenage boy sat slumped in defeat, his eyes focused on the crumpled papers in his hand. He had just failed his college exams and was envisioning the storm he'd have to weather at home. His parents would skin him alive!

The mere thought of revealing his failure was paralyzing, especially since his heart truly belonged to a different dream. He longed to be a veterinarian, nurturing and healing, not an accountant, spending each day tabulating profit and loss for the rest of his working life.

Tucked away at the far end of the café, a girl, a silent observer of the café's tapestry of struggle, leaned in closer, her eyes scanning the scene.

Her companion, ever perceptive, whispered, "The lady's frustration with her job is a reminder that we all crave meaning in our work. And the couple, well, their argument, while painful, is a sign of their commitment to finding a way through the storm together."

"And the boy?" the girl asked softly.

"The boy," he said with a gentle smile, "is a testament to the courage it takes to pursue a dream despite the fear."

"He's not alone in his struggle. Each person here is facing their battle, but it's in these shared struggles that we find our humanity."

The girl pondered this; her heart heavy with empathy.

The young waiter interrupted her thoughts as he stepped in to clear the empty cups and plates from their table. As he leaned forward, he lost his balance while trying to avoid something he thought he had accidentally stepped on beneath the table.

The plates clattered loudly, causing several patrons to turn and look at the source of the commotion. The waiter, flustered and red-faced, began apologizing profusely, his words tumbling over each other as he tried to make amends.

"So sorry," he stammered, scrambling to collect the scattered dishes.

Despite his sincere apologies, the moment quickly passed. With a few nods and murmurs of understanding, the pair resumed their observations, and the scene settled back into its previous calm.

The sun dipped below the horizon, and the café's lights flickered on, casting a warm glow over the patrons. As the café bustled with the quiet hum of evening activity, the girl and her companion shared a knowing smile.

Reevan stood up and said with conviction, "Come on, Neemo. Our job starts now."

Bob stirred from her cat nap under the table and strode elegantly out with her companion, her soft yellow eyes shining with hope.

–The End–

who is arief abdullah tan @ christopher tan?

MEET Arief @ Chris, a man whose life is a cocktail of deep musings that no one else seems to appreciate and athletic feats that have left him with two creaky knees and lungs that sound like a rusty accordion.

He made his literary debut with *Coming Through My Eyes*, published by MPH Distributors in 2010, offering a comical Malaysian take on everything from societal quirks to national progress.

He has spent the last three decades in editorial, journalism, and corporate communications... that's a whole lot of nasi lemak wrappers!

Arief holds a 'B' diploma in coaching from the Asian Football Confederation. He's also a certified Personal Development Leadership coach. With over 30 years of sporting exploits, Chris (yes, it's confusing) literally climbs mountains and run marathons.

When he's not scaling peaks, you will find him crouched in fields and sports arenas, snapping away with his t(rusty) digital SLR camera and lens that is longer than a baby giraffe's neck.

If you have any rebuttals about this book or pent-up anger from his last one, drop Arief an email at *a2comms@gmail.com*.